Gazpacho for Nacho

by
Tracey Kyle

illustrated by
Carolina Farías

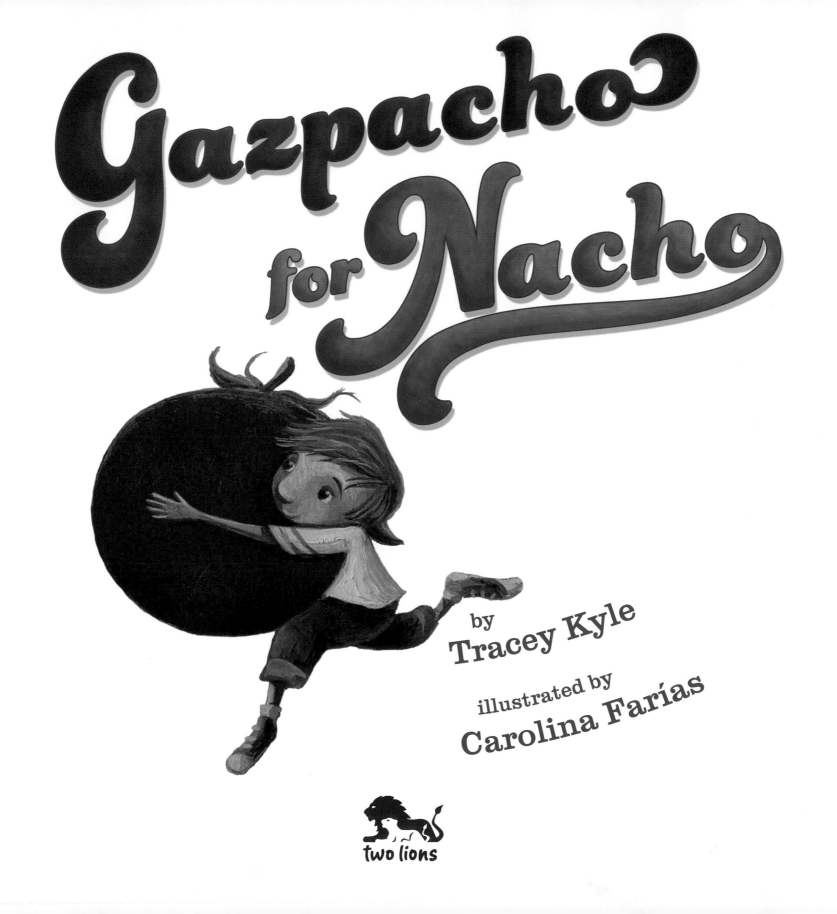

two lions

two lions

Text copyright © 2014 by Tracey Kyle
Illustrations copyright © 2014
by Amazon Children's Publishing

Amazon Publishing
Attn: Amazon Children's Publishing
P.O. Box 400818
Las Vegas, NV 89140
www.amazon.com/amazonchildrenspublishing

Library of Congress Cataloging-in-Publication Data
is available upon request.

ISBN-13: 9781477817278 (hardcover)
ISBN-10: 1477817271 (hardcover)
ISBN-13: 9781477867273 (eBook)
ISBN-10: 1477867279 (eBook)

The illustrations are rendered in a variety of mediums,
especially watercolors and acrylics.

Book design by Vera Soki
Editor: Margery Cuyler

Printed in China (R)
First edition
10 9 8 7 6 5 4 3

To Neil, for eating
everything I cook
—T.K.

To my mom,
who is like Nacho
—C.F.

In a big, big city by a large, busy *plaza*
lived a very small boy in a simple white *casa*.

The name of this tiny *muchacho* was Nacho,
and all he would eat was a soup called *gazpacho*.
Gazpacho for breakfast, *gazpacho* for lunch,
gazpacho for dinner, for snacks, and for brunch.

He didn't like meat or the smell of *pescado*.
He didn't like chicken or ice-cold *helado*!
And when he saw slices of manchego cheese,
he asked, "Is there any *gazpacho* left, please?"

Mami would say, "You're a picky *muchacho*."
Nacho would say, "But I just want *gazpacho*!"
At breakfast, he woke up to *leche* and *churros*.
He cried, "*¡Mami, ay!* This is food for the *burros*!"

For snacks, Mami sliced up *chorizo* and bread.
Nacho would ask for *gazpacho* instead.
At lunchtime, Mami served Spanish *tortilla*.
Nacho would put the pan under his *silla*.

At dinner, Mami fried mushrooms, or *setas*,
and served them with rice next to crispy *croquetas*.
She filled up a bowl with fresh loaves of *pan*
and whipped up a custard dessert she called *flan*.
All of the food was rejected by Nacho.
"Gazpacho, gazpacho!" he cried. *"¡Más gazpacho!"*

There wasn't a *plato* that Nacho would touch.
Mami grew tired from cooking so much!

"Nacho," she cried. "It's not right! *No es justo*
that all of these meals are not to your *gusto*!
You're coming with me to the market. We're shopping."
"I'm learning to cook?" Nacho asked, his eyes popping.

The market was bustling; people were looking
for all the *legumbres* they needed for cooking.
Nacho's mouth watered while gazing at piles
of colorful vegetables stretched out for miles.

Onions, potatoes: *cebollas y papas*;
bamboo and spinach: *bambú, espinacas*;
cucumbers, mushrooms: *pepinos y setas*;
lettuce and lentils: *lechuga, lentejas*;
corn, avocados: *maíz, aguacates*;
and last but not least, bright red, juicy *tomates*!

"Tomatoes," said Mami, "for you to cook, Nacho.
You'll learn to prepare your beloved *gazpacho*!"
"*¡Olé!*" Nacho cried. "I can cook! Yes I can!"
And off to the *puestos* of veggies he ran.
He gathered *tomates* that smelled fresh and clean
and found a *pepino* whose skin was dark green.

Among all the colorful, fresh *alimentos,*
he picked out a few crispy, green *pimientos*.
He added a small clove of garlic, or *ajo,*
and set off for home to begin *el trabajo.*

Dressing the part with a huge chef's *sombrero*,
Nacho felt just like a true *cocinero*.
With bright red *tomates* piled up to his chin,
he looked up at Mami and said, "Let's begin!"
They cored and they sliced and they diced and they seeded
the pounds of tomatoes and peppers they needed.

Mami then carefully chopped a *cebolla*.
Nacho helped, finding a pot, a large *olla*.
"Nacho," said Mami, "I need the *pepino*."
He gave her the cucumber. What a good *niño*!
Mami then crumbled some bread in the pot
and left it to soak till it softened a lot.

They sprinkled some *sal*, and it flew through the air.
"*¡Ay!* Nacho!" cried Mami. "The bowl's over there!"
Lastly, she drizzled a very small drop
of oil and vinegar over the top.
She blended the soup in a big *batidora*
and left it to chill in the fridge for one *hora*.

Dinner that night was a wonderful treat.
"Nacho!" called Mami, "¡*La cena!* Come eat!"
Nacho rushed into the kitchen and saw
the bowls of *gazpacho* and stood there in awe.
Bowl after bowl after bowl of *gazpacho*,
cooked by a clever, creative *muchacho*.
He sat down to eat with a giant *sonrisa*
and finished the soup very quickly—*de prisa*!

Nacho was happy, but deep in his heart,
he knew that *gazpacho* was only the start.
He thought of the fresh, tasty meals he would make,
the foods he would cook and the sweets he would bake.
Eagerly off to the kitchen he dashed,
where all the *legumbres*, the veggies, were stashed.
"Mami," he said, "though I love my *gazpacho*,
I'm trying new recipes! Call me Chef Nacho!"

YUMMY-IN-THE-TUMMY GAZPACHO

1 28-ounce can of diced tomatoes
1 large cucumber
1 green pepper
¼ teaspoon garlic powder

¼ teaspoon onion powder
3 tablespoons olive oil
1 tablespoon red or sherry vinegar
1 teaspoon salt

1. Pour the tomatoes and their juice into a medium-sized mixing bowl.

2. With an adult's help, chop the cucumber and pepper into small pieces.

3. Add the chopped cucumber and green pepper to the bowl of tomatoes.

4. Add the garlic powder, onion powder, olive oil, vinegar, and salt to the mixture.

5. Chill in the refrigerator for 1 hour. Serve in six small bowls.

6. Optional: Add dried croutons to the top.

GLOSSARY

(los) aguacates (Lohs-ah-guah-KAH-tehs)
avocados

(el) ajo (Ehl-AH-hoh) garlic

(los) alimentos (Lohs-ah-lee-MEHN-tohs)
food

¡Ay! (AH-y) Oh dear!

(el) bambú (Ehl-bahm-BOO) bamboo

(la) batidora (Lah-bah-tee-DOH-rah) mixer

(los) burros (Lohs-BOO-rohs) donkeys

(la) casa (Lah-KAH-sah) house

(las) cebollas (Lahs-seh-BOH-yahs)
onions

(la) cena (Lah-SAY-nah) dinner

(el) chorizo (Ehl-choh-REE-soh) A pork
sausage

(los) churros (Lohs-CHOO-rohs) Thin
strips of dough deep-fried in olive oil and
sprinkled with sugar

(el) cocinero (Ehl-koh-see-NEH-roh) cook
/ chef

(las) croquetas (Lahs-kroh-KEH-tas)
croquettes (small, oval-shaped cakes
normally filled with potatoes and meat,
fish, and/or vegetables; they are coated
in bread crumbs and sautéed in olive oil.)

de prisa (Deh-PREE-sah) quickly

(las) espinacas (Lahs-eh-spee-NAH-kahs)
spinach

(el) flan (Ehl-flahn) a baked custard with
a caramel glaze

(el) gazpacho (Ehl-gahs-PAH-cho) a
cold, tomato-based vegetable soup that
originated in Andalucía, Spain

(el) gusto (Ehl-GOO-stoh) liking/taste

(el) helado (Ehl-eh-LAH-doh) ice cream

(la) hora (Lah-OH-rah) hour

(la) leche (Lah-LEH-cheh) milk

(la) lechuga (Lah-leh-CHOO-gah) lettuce

(los) legumbres (Lohs-leh-GOOM-brehs)
vegetables

(las) lentejas (Lahs-lehn-TEH-hahs)
lentils

(el) maíz (Ehl-mah-EES) corn

Más (MAHS) more

(el) muchacho (Ehl-moo-CHAH-choh) boy

(el) niño (Ehl-NEEN-yoh) little boy

Nacho (NAH-choh) a common nickname
for the Spanish name Ignacio

No es justo (No-ehs-HOO-stoh) It's not fair

¡Olé! (Oh-LEH) Yeah!

(la) olla (Lah-OH-yah) large pot

(el) pan (Ehl-PAHN) bread

(las) papas (Lahs-PAH-pahs) potatoes

(el) pepino (Ehl-peh-PEE-noh) cucumber

(el) pescado (Ehl-peh-SKAH-doh) fish

(los) pimientos (Lohs-pee-mee-YEN-tohs)
peppers

(el) plato (Ehl-PLAH-toh) dish; meal

(la) plaza (Lah-PLAH-sah) the main public
square

(los) puestos (Lohs-PWEH-stos) stalls (at
the market)

(el) sal (Ehl-SAHL) salt

(las) setas (Lahs-SEH-tahs) mushrooms

(la) silla (Lah-SEE-yah) chair

(el) sombrero (Ehl-sohm-BREH-roh) hat

(la) sonrisa (Lah-son-REE-sah) smile

(los) tomates (Lohs-toh-MAH-tehs)
tomatos

(la) tortilla (Lah-tohr-TEE-yah) a potato,
egg, and onion omelet

(el) trabajo (Ehl-trah-BAH-hoh) work

y (EE) and